Apples for Sale

ISBN 0 86112 585 1
© Brimax Books Ltd 1989
All rights reserved
Published by Brimax Books Ltd, Newmarket, England 1989
Printed in Italy

Apples for Sale

by Lucy Kincaid

Illustrated by Eric Kincaid

Brimax Books · Newmarket · England

The apples on the apple tree are ripe.
It is time to pick them.

"I will hold the ladder steady," says Pipkin.

Grandpa is going to sell some apples.
First he must put up a stall.

Grandpa takes the apples out of the barrel.
Pipkin puts a shine on the apples.

"Grandma is calling me," says Grandpa.
"I will look after the stall," says Pipkin.

"Apples for sale!" shouts Pipkin.
He hopes someone comes along soon.

Everyone comes to buy apples.
Pipkin is very busy.

Grandpa is gone a long time.
Pipkin sells all the apples.

Little Tom has run a long way.
"Can I buy one of your apples?" he asks.

"Is there one left in the barrel?" asks Tom.
"I will look," says Pipkin.

Pipkin stands on his tiptoes. He can see
an apple. He cannot quite reach it.

"I have it!" shouts Pipkin. And then
he falls head first into the barrel.

The barrel wobbles. It falls over.
It begins to roll. Pipkin is still inside it.

Grandpa hears Tom Rabbit shouting.
Grandpa comes running.
"What is wrong?" shouts Grandpa.

"Stop! Stop!" shouts Grandpa.
"Stop! Stop!" shouts Tom Rabbit.

"I would if I could!" shouts Pipkin
from inside the barrel.

"Where am I going?" shouts Pipkin
as he flies into the air.

"Into the pond!" shouts Grandpa.
What a big splash Pipkin makes.

Pipkin is wet and very dizzy.
But what is he holding?

"This is the best apple I have ever tasted,"
says Tom.
"Well done Pipkin!" says Grandpa.